# ZAHRA'S

# FANTASIES

# ZAHRA'S

# FANTASIES

ALEX

Woven Words Publishers OPC Pvt. Ltd.

Registered Office:

Vill: Raipur, P.O: Raipur Paschimbar,

Dist: Purba Midnapore, Pin: 721401,

West Bengal, India.

www.wovenwordspublishers.in

Email: editor@wovenwordspublishers.in

First published by Woven Words Publishers OPC Pvt. Ltd., 2018

NOVEL

IMPRINT: WOVEN WORDS RED

ISBN 13: 978-93-86897-27-5

ISBN 10: 938689727X

Price: ₹150/$6

Printed and bound in India

# CHAPTER ONE

Zahra Khamdi Asaidi lived inside high walls, where there was no lack since she was eighteen. She was a happy woman. Her children had all grown up and her first three daughters were married. She was indeed blessed. If it were possible to have it all, then she was one person that had it all. Her son who is also her last child were now in a university in North Carolina, United States of America. Khamdi, her husband, a real estate developer had it all going for him. Life was good with this couple. Khamdi left his mansion occasionally and went to his realtor's office where he chatted and spent his time relaxing. His mansion was now thirty years old; a relish of the past. Khamdi was now getting ready to give his house a face lift and needed to get a general assessment of his house. Zahra was in the kitchen with Aisha, her house help, a humble Ethiopian girl. They were making lunch when Khamdi came home to do his assessment. Zahra and Aisha were like friends. There was peace and harmony between them. Aisha had gone to get something outside when they heard a loud scream. It was Khamdi from their bedroom. Zahra was shocked and it was at the point she was bringing down her soup from fire. Out of the shock, the pot fell down and the soup spilled on the flow with splashes of hot soup on her face. She screamed as she reached for the tap to wash her face. Once Aisha heard her katil(boss) shout, she threw the broom she was holding and started to run upstairs to find out what had happened to her boss. Then she heard another scream from her madam. She was just passing the kitchen to reach upstairs but she instantly diverted and went to find out what had happened to her madam. She met her scrambling and trying to turn on the tap. She scattered everything on the kitchen cabinet while trying to do this. Aisha helped her with the tap and went to the guest bathroom and brought a towel for her. While all these were going on, Khamdi was still shouting lai e la e la la and his voice getting louder. Zahra in her pains ordered Aisha to go and find out what was wrong with her husband. Aisha was the most confused at that moment. Her boss has never raised his voice in her 3 years of service at their house.

She then went before her boss and he didn't even talk to her but only asked that she should call her madam. She kept mute and watched the man. He was holding something in his hands but she couldn't see it clearly. All she could see was a paper and her boss kept shouting lai e la e la la. She explained to him that her madam was hurt but he wanted to see her immediately so without much wait, he followed Aisha downstairs. But Aisha in her curiosity wanted to see what he was holding in his hand. When she made out that it was a torn packet of condom. She screamed eeh. Khalid looked back. He knew she made a sound but was unsure. He asked her why had she shouted. She kept quiet and pretended there was nothing. When they got to the kitchen, he was surprised the way he saw his wife. Her face was reddish and she was still in pains. When he got closer, he saw that there were blisters, scabs and abrasions. She was still in pains. He reached to touch her face but she moved away. He forcibly touched it and she screamed in pains this time louder than before. He was scared. He unconsciously threw away the condom pack as he went upstairs to get his mobile phone. He called his driver on phone. He lived at the security apartment which was quite a distance from the main building. The Pakistani driver rushed in with the urgency in the tone of the call he had received and together they all took Zahra to the hospital. She was old with the spirit of a youth. While they rode in their latest Armada jeep, Zahra asked her husband why he had shouted. He pretended not to have heard what she said. She went on to narrate to him how she lost control of the pot of soup she was carrying because of his shout. She had thought something terrible happened to her husband. While in the hospital she was given analgesics and sedative. Her wound was dressed. She was discharged later that day with a bandage that covered her entire face, sparing her eyes, just in the usual fashion she covered her face with a niqab. At home, Khamdi refused to talk about his discovery but Aisha had told Zahra all she observed. They weren't only madam and maid anymore but were partners in the unconventional events of the Khamdi mansion. As Zahra lay in pains she began to play the entire scene in her mind.

# CHAPTER TWO

Khamdi and Zahra had visited all the cities in the world. They took their annual vacation abroad. Six years ago in a hotel in California, a strange drunk black man bumped onto Zahra on the hotel corridor. She was walking back to their hotel room when this tall and muscular black guy fell on her with all his weight. She was struggling to help him up and free herself. The guy, obviously drunk, was saying 204, 204,204. Zahra didn't understand nor speak English unlike her husband. She knew the English numbers enough to know her phone numbers and she knew her room in the hotel was 206. Frustrated and angered by the smell of alcohol and the fact he was holding an alcoholic drink, she couldn't wait to free herself from this strange man. The hotel lobby was long and there was no help in sight. She feared that forcibly pushing the man away might lead to him suffering some injuries. At the same time she wasn't that young or strong to support his weight for too long. When she got oriented of her location, she realized that room 204 was the next room from where they were standing and hers adjacent to it. She tried to support the man as he leaned on her till they got to his door. He didn't have his key. She put her hands in his right pocket and brought out the electronics card key. As she opened the door the man was by this time sleeping on her shoulder. With all the energy she could muster, she led him inside his room. During the struggle the man retched and vomited on her. With anger and frustration, she pushed him on the bed and rushed to use the telephone to call for help. But she was still holding the phone directory and wondering what number to call. She could only read the numbers but not what they were for. Her only knowledge of English was the numbers and possibly how to say you are welcome, thank you and hi. However she couldn't read any other thing in English. While still holding the phone directory and also wondering the implication of her husband finding out she was in a man's room, the man began to grunt for assistance. She helped him remove his shoes. He was struggling to remove his jean trousers without unfastening the button. She helped him do this. While unfastening his belt she pinched his abdomen with the iron head of the belt. He whimpered. She tried apologizing. But then again, the sight of the penis through the boxers was inviting. She touched the penis, then again and again and again, till it became turgid. She quickly helped him remove his jeans and was to leave. But she hadn't seen the penis of a black man before, not even in the movies. She thought this was her opportunity. She believed that this will be harmless flirtation since the man was drunk and weak. The turgid penis was pushing through the boxers. She watched in awe and marveled at the size of it. She wondered how a woman would enjoy that for she thought it too big for comfort. She had had five children, seen many things in her world but the size of this black man's penis was still a wonder to her. Before she could realize what she was doing she had pulled it out of the boxers and was holding the dick and laughing. She indeed thought herself as a child with no thought of consequences of her actions. The man was still struggling in his drowsiness and muttering nonsense. Suddenly while holding the penis, the man held her and was urging her to hold the dick harder. She now knew she was in the wrong place but couldn't help herself anymore. She was enjoying herself and didn't think of anything other than plainly playing with her new found toy. The man was still muttering incoherently and suddenly she realized he had gripped her forcefully. She was sitting on the bed. there was little time left for her to put up any resistance as he pushed her down on the bed, raised her abaya and began to reach out for her most private parts that no other man but her husband has ever reached. She was saying la la la (no no) but she could no longer put any firm hesitation for she feared she could alert the neighbors but mostly because she enjoyed the act. He yanked off her pants with so much speed that she hardly could tell what happened. She knew what was happening could earn her a death sentence but she had no will to stop it. Her only wish was that it could happen fast and her prayer was that no one will find out. She earnestly prayed that her husband will spend more time with the new friends he made in the hotel, time enough to enable her come out of her dream world. When she looked up, he was sliding his turgid dick inside her wet pussy. She was surprised as she expected some pain but all she felt was pleasure. She wondered why she didn't feel any pain this time. Sex with her husband was often painful. Her husband was a man moderately endowed. How could this large sized cucumber bring this pleasure when she expected only pain? The result she expected was mere adventure. To have something stupid she had done in her lifetime, but this was totally unexpected. For a moment she liked it, in another moment she hated herself for not stopping it. She had never done anything unexpected of a Muslim woman all her life. Zahra was an example for any Muslim woman to emulate. Young men who were newly married brought their wives to her so she could teach them how to be a good Muslim wife. Nearly two thirds of her childhood friends were either in their third of forth marriage or divorced. Everyone wanted to know her charm. How she managed to remain the only wife of a wealthy Muslim man. While the world wondered about Zahra's secrets she was by that time screaming and crying in ecstasy. She was urging the man to push harder and faster. The only thing she could associate with her present experience was when she newly married her husband. Even that was a far cry to what she was enjoying. She would raise her legs and spread it out and wrap it around the man. He was pounding hard and fast and they were both sweating though the air conditioner was on. Suddenly she jerked, screamed loud and felt like a part of her left, and she passed out. She was only awaked with the constant thrust that didn't last long as the man climaxed. She was too tired and all her muscles were so relaxed that she didn't realize she was sleeping until she was awakened by the man. She hurriedly stood up and reached for her bags and ran out of the room. She only realized she had left her panties in the man's room when she had finished taking her bath and wanted to wash her pants.

# CHAPTER THREE

As she took her bath, she scrubbed hard and long. She was in tears. With each weep she scrubbed even harder as though she wanted to peel off her skin. She earnestly wanted to wash off all the sinful touch. She came into the room folded her abaya and her cloth of sin and wrapped them in one of the used nylon from their previous day shopping. She thought of her panties but was somewhat grateful she had left it in his room. She had no intention of ever seeing or touching any item of clothing she wore before her encounter with the strange man. When the husband came in she had cried herself to sleep. Her eyes however left some trace that something was wrong with her. As the husband reached to touch her and have a feel of her he noticed she had been crying. He asked her what was the problem but she pretended to be far asleep. Khamdi held his wife from behind oblivious of all that had transpired. He was horny and tried to urge her for sex. In her deeply asleep pretence, she wanted to please her husband as a way of paying for her sins but she felt too dirty and guilty. She believed that letting her husband touch her would be letting him share from her sins. In her sincerity, she desired to pay for her sins alone. She also feared that he might find out she slept out if he had sex with her that night. She was unsure if her long hours of washing and crying got rid of all the traces. She had washed her vagina countless times in her effort to remove all the sperm. She had forced her hand inside her vagina to wash off everything. She even wrapped a cloth with water and soap and put inside her vagina while trying to clean herself of the biological products of the infidel. Despite all these efforts she was still uncertain she was clean enough to let her husband of twenty-eight years have sex with her. The ensuing days were so depressing for Zahra and she demanded that they left the hotel for another. She was unsure if the strange man was still next door but she wanted to avoid anything that will remind her of the man. She was so insecure in that hotel. She didn't know how she would react if she saw the man again and the thought that she might let him have her if he asked for it made her more depressed. By the evening, of the following day, Khamdi was no longer enjoying his wife's gloomy look. He thought the problem was that he rebuffed her when she suggested that they leave the hotel or the prompting for sex the previous night. Determined to improve on her mood in order to have sex with her that night, he promised her that they would check into another hotel at dawn. She thanked him and tried to act happy but inside she knew the problem was with what she did and not where they were. Khamdi didn't succeed in getting the loving care he had always enjoyed with his wife. The only secret to their long happy marriage was her constant willingness to please her husbands' sexual desire. Khamdi knew something serious was wrong but of a million choices his mind did not go to the possibility of another man holding his wife's hand and someone having sex with his wife was an unthinkable thought. By the fifth day, Khamdi was totally frustrated and woke up shouting at Zahra. He urged her to pack her things for he was going to call his ticket agent for their return. He succeeded in getting a ticket for the next day and their holiday was interrupted as they returned to Khamdi mansion. In Khamdi's mansion, things were never the same again. The thought of the strange man, how she met him and all that transpired was all Zahra could think of. She played that thought in her head more often than she prayed. Praying and saying her *subha* had been her main companion all her life. But then she had welcomed another. When she was not thinking of that she was worried of the guilt. She thought of confessing the incident to her husband but was unsure how he would react. She found herself severally trying to confess that deed to someone but often she held herself back. She knew of the grim consequences that could follow if she did. She could be put to death. She indeed would be put to death if the story went public. For that fear she chose to live in her depression than risk death. In all her awareness, she had committed the unforgivable. She knew talking to somebody would help her guilt state but she didn't have anyone to trust with it. Not because it was impossible to have a friend who could conceal her secret but in her case she was the angel in everyone's sight. Only angels or intending ones would dare to come close to her. She was so depressed that one day she called Aisha into her room and began to tell her what happened in the hotel. The pressure she had borne all those years was so much she feared she could go mad if she continued to keep all to herself. She had that burden all by herself for three years before they employed Aisha and it took her another one year to decide if she was the one to confide in.

# CHAPTER FOUR

Aisha was married in her village in Ethiopia. She had been a Muslim until she met a Christian man in Saudi who she fell in love with and she became a Christian. Her identification card still read Muslim. Zahra believed her to be a Muslim despite all her insistence that she wasn't anymore. She needed the counsel of a Muslim woman to understand how she would come out of her guilt. If only she kept her sins to herself. Talking to Aisha was the beginning of her many woes. Aisha was a sexually liberated woman. Zahras' story only amused her for even though she just turned thirty she couldn't imagine how a woman would have slept with only one man until a holiday in her 56th year of life. Aisha repeated Zahra's story to her only making it more erotic and seem exciting. Zahra began to enjoy the thoughts of a day she had thought of as her most horrible day. Zahra never knew the name of the man she had slept with, where he was from and nothing about him. All she remembered was 204. In their stories, 204 became their code of talking about the incident. When they are not discussing the size of 204's dick, they are talking of the erotic scenes and action. Zahra completely forgot her guilt after she started discussing the incident with Aisha.

This was partly because of how Aisha switched the stories from a horrible one to an exciting one. Also the stories of Aisha's numerous sexual experiences left Zahra feeling cheated and deprived. Zahra did not realize how much she had transformed until she began to fantasize of being with a black man. By that time, while she drove to the mall, the sight of any black man got her instantly wet. She practically died every time she saw a clean black man. She only had two simple thought that kept her busy; her encounter with 204 and the thought of making out with a black man. Aisha knew only of the first but didn't know how badly her madam fantasizes of a repeat experience. One day in their routine chats, Zahra asked Aisha "Do you know any black man with a big dick?" In her many thoughts and reminiscing about the 204 incident she had come to believe that the magic to her exhilarating sexual experience was in the size. Aisha was not into blacks anymore. She had grown wise and felt that her fellow Africans were only out for sexual pleasures without giving back. She was into men who help her financially. Though she was the lowest in social strata in Saudi but in her village she was highly respected. She had built a house for her family and was then building one for herself and her brother. To do these huge projects she needed Arab money, she wasn't going to waste any time with Ethiopian drivers, Kenyan gardener or Nigerian car wash-men. Her last kafil after sleeping with her wanted his friends to experience the sweet pussy of an African maid. It was the money she got from these men that made her a queen in her village. However Aisha had a boyfriend named Monday, the only Blackman she makes out with. She has grown attached to him but was not willing to discuss her madam's request with him. She also wasn't sure if Monday was as big as her madam had described, but what plaque her thought more was why her madam asked about big black dick. She told her madam she didn't know anyone. Zahra told Aisha what turned her on and how frustrated she got when her husband could not met up with her new sexual height. By that time Zahra was in her early sixties only, her sexual urge was like that of a young girl in her twenties. Her best friend now was Aisha and all they ever talk of was sex. Aisha liked to make her madam happy and was going to find her a black man. Her only worry now was if she could share Monday with her madam but other than jealousy she was also unsure how her madam would react when she would discover that she had passed on her left over. Aisha thought that Zahra could get jealous if she learnt she was sharing a man with her maid. Aisha asked Monday if he had black friends with big dicks but didn't tell him about her discussion with Zahra. Monday did not offer any help with this. Aisha's perception of black men was that those in menial jobs where better endowed. She was a bold and daring woman. She had heard the story of 204 severally that she could recognize him if she ever saw him. Her mission now was to find someone with the same look and hope he would be similarly endowed.

# CHAPTER FIVE

When Aisha went to visit her sister in Bawadi, a highly populated area in town, she went to a car wash. The car wash was big and the workers were mainly young black men. Aisha's sister Nadia was a common prostitute. She could have sex for anything just provided it was money. She was at that time known in her neighborhood as 50 riyal. That was what she mostly charged her Pakistani customers. A few blacks patronize Nadia but she knew nothing about those men. She could be taking up the task of finding a big black dick though she has had many. Aisha and Nadia were together at the car wash. It was there that Aisha saw a tall Blackman. He had tiny dreads, slim with small buttocks at the same time muscular. He looked much like 204. She called the guy and told him she had something to discuss with him. The man was scared for Aisha was fully covered sparing only her eyes. That was not compulsory in this area of town where women were allowed to leave their hair bare. He imagined what he could possibly discuss with this extreme conservative lady. Women did not talk to men but women dressed like that were the kind who would leave a room simply because a man walked into it. Aisha wasted no time to spill the beans. The man was shocked at a conservative woman asking him about his penis. Aisha could see the surprise on his face. She told him you really need to answer me because that might be all you need to get out of the hot sun "you could make a lot of money than what you make washing cars under the sun in a month." He answered her that he thought he had what she might be looking for and urged her to state the deal. She took his number and assured him that she would call him. She was by this time wondering if believing him was the right thing to do. How was she going to confirm what he had said was true. She really wouldn't want to disappoint her madam. They were leaving the car wash when the man called Nadia by a strange name and asked her if she wasn't the one staying at no 6 Abdallah roads. Nadia didn't like been accosted by men for often they were men she met in her line of trade. That was exactly how he knew Nadia. They have both traded on pleasure before. Nadia forced herself to look at him and could recall she had met him. It was not usual to recall the men she had been with but she did that time because their encounter didn't end well. She had a fight with Hawsawe because she could not stand the long painful sex and demanded her money before the end of the act. They however settled and completed their business. But, it was in that time between their fights and finally going on to complete their deal that she was able to observe him enough and that was why she then recognized him. Nadia walked away not accepting she knew him but was honest with Aisha that indeed Hawsawe was endowed. Aisha informed her madam of Hawsawe. She was excited. She didn't have any plan but was willing to do whatever it took to have the 204 experience again. Jointly they tried to come up with a plan. She could put him in a hotel and met him there. Aisha informed her of the hotel cameras and how she always beat the cameras by covering her entire face if she became scared someone could recognize her by her eye. Zahra believed it was a great plan. She was used to covering and nothing would feel different for her. She was so sure that there would be no better plan than that. She was however worried about something – how she would get there? Taxis were no easy option since she had a driver. She would have to pretend she was going to the shop, enter the mall and exit from another gate and board a taxi to her fantasy location. That was her best plan. She was already fascinating on how to do all these in her sixties. They had concluded on the plan when Aisha asked her if it was possible to employ a male steward. Aisha hated been sent to wash the water tank and since she became close to her madam she had been able to voice this out to her. Washing the tank entailed climbing the ladder and she was so scared the first time she had to do that. It was a manly task. She had gotten use to it, but still hated the chore. That was her opportunity to get help. The only reason why she had been the one doing it was because her madam felt it was indecent to allow a male non relative inside their compound. She couldn't imagine being seen by a male. For that reason, no males were allowed within Khamdi castle. The drivers only entered the compound when called for a trip. She had never allowed any discussion on employing a male worker. For that reason, her children all partook in the house chores. Her sons had been the ones helping with washing of the water tank before they left for their university. Now Aisha did the chore with lots of grumbling. Aisha suggested to her madam that they could employ Hawsawe. This would give a perfect alibi and remove all suspicion from Khamdi, the public or anyone that might be watching. That day Zahra gave Aisha a diamond wrist band that her husband bought for her 15 years ago. The price tag on this wrist band was 30000 riyal but her excitement didn't let her evaluate what she was giving to a common maid. Their plan was perfect. Zahra only added that they will claim that Hawsawe was Aishas husband. That was to eliminate every suspicion should anyone arise later.

All that Khamdi needed to approve a male worker in the castle was his wife's approval. If Zahra would let it, then Khamdi certainly would.

# CHAPTER SIX

Hawsawe had just two official tasks to do, wash the water tank and to sweep the compounds. Aisha was to concentrate on the chores inside the house. Hawsawe accepted both the official and the unofficial jobs happily. He was so thankful with Aisha for her omen of good luck. Hawsawe however had only one condition that he would had to use condom. He wasn't so pleased with the idea of making out with a woman in her sixties. Use of condom made the idea less offensive to him. He was however grateful to be taken from the sun. He left the most difficult job to one he could only describe as pleasure and pay. In his pleasure and pay job, he had only one thing to worry about, the fear of losing his life. He knows very well the consequences of been caught in this. The rule was clear, the married who involved in extra marital affairs were to be put to death by stoning; only the single will be flogged publicly. However that rule was of the highest consequences for non Saudis or Saudis of the second category. Black Saudis often fell in the second category. Hawsawe was a Nigerian migrant. He was born in Saudi of his hausa immigrant parents. He had every reason to worry about being illegal. He had no chances of being protected from the stringent rules should he be caught in the web of the law. Hawsawe lay on his mat in a small security house where he shares with 4 of his colleagues and thought of the grim possibilities that could befall him should something go wrong. He had heard many stories of women who were caught in the forbidden act and how more often than not the women wriggled out of it by alleging rape. Nothing was impossible in a case between a Saudi and a non Saudi. The Saudi was always right in any such case unless God decreed otherwise. Hawsawe knew he could not count on God on this. His worries were however made light when he thought of his job. The commands he got and the fact that he washed cars under the sun. Sometimes he would re-wash a car twice in order to satisfy a difficult customer. For all this he was only able to feed, sleep on a mat and use an air condition that hardly work past a week before repairs. Sometimes he and his five roommates would have to go weeks without an airconditioner. They would sleep only by having to put a moist blanket on their bare body to cope with the effect of the extreme heat. He knew that any life will be better than the one he lives. He had even contemplated committing a crime and going to prison all in the effort of escaping the hardship. He was convinced that the living conditions in prison were better than his, except that he occasionally visits Nadia and her likes. This sexual exploits was impossible if he were put in jail. However, the only reason he failed to take this option of going to prison was because the crime he thought of committing was theft and the punishment for it wasn't only prison but the loss of one arm or both. Hawsawe was sure he would certainly take his pleasure and pay job. Anything was worth it if it was going to take him off the street. By the time, Hawsawe hadn't met her madam and sex boss. All communications were on phone with Aisha. He hadn't even heard his madam's voice. He wondered what she would look like. He prayed she would be pretty although he was quite unable to imagine how a woman in her sixties would be that pretty to appeal to him. For him it was a slave job. He was the sex slave and his madam the sex boss. Hawsawe never asked Aisha how he would be remunerated. He believed that a rich women's tip was worth more than his week of earning. He knew he would have to eat a rich man's food, stay in a rich man's house and fuck a rich mans wife. Hawsawe was already fantasizing on meeting his sex boss. He ironed his best clothes and went to the popular 5 riyal market and bought a perfume. He only recalled using a perfume when he was young and his father would spray him and his siblings perfume on ed kabir (Muslim celebration) day. He went to have a haircut and do his beard. He was fully ready and now waiting for Aisha's call. The call came after three days and by the time Zahra had gotten the full approval of her husband. Hawsawe wore his clothes and raced to Khamdi castle. When he came in, Zahra was upstairs. He waited for a while preferring to stand than seat. Khamdi castle was the most magnificent thing Hawsawe had ever seen all his life. He felt uncomfortable sitting but when he became tired of standing he leaned on the wall. He spent a lot of time admiring the beautiful colored lights. The lights were well arranged and of differing color, each serving a different purpose. The inside of Khamdi castle was designed in a way that only the switch on the wall determined the look of the day. At different occasions the house took different looks depending on the choice of light for that day. The seats were made of water impermeable fabric and wool. The large sitting room had different upholstery with each look presenting a different scenario and culture, from the rich Arabian fabric to the French and Italian furniture. Everything in Khamdi castle was exquisite.

Zahra was upstairs. She was aware that Hawsawe was around and she was beginning to wonder if her little fantasy was worth the risk. She worried about heaven and God but mostly she worried about Khamdi and her children. A part of her would tell her that her planned exploits was not worth it but Aisha's voice would interrupt her thoughts. Aisha always told her "Madam you have served your husband only with your body and served your children also, this is your only time to serve yourself." Aisha had a unique way of making nonsense of Zahra's thoughts and strives to be better. Since the day she discussed 204 with Aisha her idiosyncrasy was remodeled.

# CHAPTER SEVEN

She came downstairs to meet Hawsawe. When she was half way down the staircase, she could perceive a mordant scent. When she finally met with Hawsawe, she was already very uncomfortable with the offensive odour from Hawsawe perfume. She asked him his name. He stuttered as he managed to say his name. Zahra had no intention of continuing the conversation as she felt choked from the fragrance of Hawsawe perfume. She only asked him one more question, "I hope you know why you are here. As humble as a lamb he answered in affirmative. Zahra bid farewell and went upstairs. Aisha was there all the while the conversation went on. She knew her madam well to know when she was not pleased. She was worried that her worst fears had come to fruition. She was really surprised that her madam didn't like Hawsawe. Hawsawe was tall, with the right masculine curves. No one would be unimpressed with his looks. Unless handsome were to mean something other than looks, Hawsawe was a handsome man. He was ruffled a bit which was not strange considering his type of job. Hawsawe also noticed he failed his interview and was worried if he would ever be in the castle again. Aisha reassured him that she was going to find out what was the problem and he would be on the job soon. With that assurance he left though with little hope. Zahra did not come downstairs the entire evening of that day, leaving Aisha to worry through the night. When she finally came down, she called Aisha and her first words were "Aisha I like him but tell him that if he ever comes here again he must not wear that perfume of his. She brought out some money and told Aisha "You should know by now what I like. Buy him some clothes and a nice perfume." From her talks, Aisha was sure that she was ready to serve herself with Hawsawe. Hawsawe arrived at Khamdi castle on the first day of work and was introduced to Khamdi as the new house keeper and Khamdi had a brief chat with him mainly about their family. He took him round the compound showing him parts of the house that have been poorly tended since his sons left for school. They agree on what was adequate pay for Hawsawe and he left for his office. At the office, Khamdi was uneasy and when he slept he had a dream about Hawsawe. Though his dream was obscure but he had a bad feeling about his new domestic help. Khamdi was not a man that made arbitrary decision. When he related this story to his friend Majid, he made Khamdi really fear for his acceptance of Hawsawe in his house. Nothing in their conversation had sexual content or insinuation. Zahra was beyond being thought of in a dirty way by anyone that knew her. The fear was mainly of security and theft. Majid even suggested to Khamdi that he could occasionally get paid labour to do the works Aisha would be unable to do. However Khamdi dispelled the thought of ill since they had worked with Aisha for 3 years and Hawsawe was none other than Aisha's husband. In Khamdi mansion, Hawsawe was busy performing his official duties. He climbed to the tank and washed it. He was very tired for the day was sunny. Sunny in Saudi Arabia meant burning. It was that season of the year when government officially disallowed any outdoor physical work. This rule only affected mainly those in the construction works. No one ever went into homes to ensure no physical exerting jobs are done inside. Exhausted and tire, he went to drink water from the water dispenser in the lobby. It was there that he slept off. He was putting on only boxers as demanded by the duty he just completed. Zahra had come downstairs because she heard a cat *meow*. They didn't own cats but because of their large compounds and rich waste collections, they entertained wild cats occasionally. Zahra hated cats and always demanded that Aisha should chase the cats from the compound. She was coming down to chase them herself but on getting down she saw that Aisha was already doing that. She could also see the bare body of Hawsawe. She tried to count the abdominal lines. His muscles were beautifully partitioned into compartments. She stood and was admiring Hawsawe while he lay on the rugged floor sleeping. She came closer and took a long thorough look at Hawsawe, wondering why blacks had this compartmentalized body she admired. She went back upstairs and when she came down she was practically naked wearing only a purple see through night gown, she last wore more than a decade ago. She came out to talk to Aisha. Once Aisha saw her madam she knew what her next role was. Before Zahra could say anything she nodded and went outside.

Khamdi castle had a large aviary at its entrance. Its environment was monitored for the birds were from different continents and needed varied environmental conditions to survive. The aviary had canaries, finches, parrots, love birds and many African and Australian birds. That was the closest part of the castle to the frequently used entrance. The other two gates were only open at occasions like during the wedding ceremony of the Khamdi daughters. Aisha went to the aviary. She would be there until Hawsawe came to exchange her. She loved staying in the aviary but that time she would have to stay there more not out of her desire but of responsibility to help conceal the immoral affairs in Khamdi mansion. Her duty there was to know when Khamdi was returning and to alert her madam of his return so that she could clear the house of anything suspicious of immoral act in Khamdi mansion. Inside, Zahra lay on top of Hawsawe. He was startled awake but Zahra put crossed her index finger on her lips and whispered a silent shhhhhhhhhhh. Hawsawe stayed calm as Zahra was now rocking herself from side to side on Hawsawe bare body. Hawsawe dick was now erect and as Zahra lay rocking his body, she grabbed his erect dick with her thigh and was wriggling her thigh and buttocks. Hawsawe was now fully ready to perform any sexual function that might be needed but he had no condom with him as the condom was in his pocket. Condom was not Zahra's idea but Hawsawe's. In fact she knew nothing of condom but the stories that some young girls got condoms stuck in their bodies during sex and were taken to the hospital to have it removed. Hawsawe could not wriggle out of her madams body and hadn't the boldness to interrupt her enjoyment for any reason. Zahra had spent some time watching some erotic video clips shown to her by Aisha. In their sexual fantasy talks pornography was a constant part of it. Zahra knew that pornography was not allowed in Saudi and it surprised her that Aisha had loads of them downloaded and sent to her from her more liberal country. Zahra always asked Aisha for new ones. She kept herself updated with it. She was now practicing her learnt skill on Hawsawe. She would grab Hawsawe's scrotum, holding it like an egg she would gently run her five fingers round it. Then she used her nails to write on the balls. Hawsawe was getting extreme pleasure from this as he lay supine and helpless on the floor. Zahra was busy inventing techniques she learnt only previously from Aishas porn collections. While she was busy touching all the erotic sites of

Hawsawe's, she put her index finger in his mouth for him to play with. She would hold his penis in her hands and squeeze it hardly. And then she began to run her hands on his erect penis like he was milking a cow. She lay back on his body and whispered "follow me." She went straight to the leather sofa preferring this for its coldness. As she sat on the sofa, she opened her legs widely. One leg made a full 90 degrees and the other was flexed and hanging on the arm rest of the sofa. She took Hawsawe's hands and put it in her pussy. He was now fondling her pussy as he liked. He would play guitar with her clitoris on one hand while the other was inside her pussy and ran it through the walls. She was now making some guttural groans and this made Hawsawe to increase his tempo and speed. Then he knelt down and began to stimulate her more with his tongues. He would fold his tongue as though he were forming a pipe with it. Using the tip of the piped tongue he would tickle her clitoris. He makes several shapes with his tongue as he did this. She was in the height of ecstasy as Hawsawe struggled to make a lasting impression. While this was going on she reached climax but the continued stimulation put her back in the mood. She could no longer stand the stimulation so she asked him to take her immediately. He stood and spread his legs as he plugged his huge penis gently inside her. He would forcefully thrust in, hold it for a while and pull out gently then making another forceful thrust inside. After some time, his thrust were now more regular but still gentle and suddenly he was pounding her in the fastest possibly was he could and they were both screaming and making animal noises. She stopped him and made a horse position. A stunt she had watched recently, realizing she is too old for this she reached for the back rest of the sofa and laid her chest on it leaving her exposed pussy for Hawsawe to rock and roll. Suddenly Hawsawes thrust became so irreugular and his jerks were now uncontrollable. Zahra pulled out and he held his dick strongly and jerked until his full load of sperm was spattered on the rugs. Zahra had climax severally during the thrust. Zahra lay straight on the long couch and Hawsawe ran to the kitchen and got a wet towel and began to scrub the floor to remove his sperm and any trace of it from the rug. His sex boss was now snoring as she lay naked on the couch. He took time to clean the entire house and sprayed deodorant though the house had air fresheners hanged all over.

# CHAPTER EIGHT

This event became almost a daily occurrence in Khamdi mansion. They affair made Zahra more vocal and the husband would notice her gay spirit and wondered what had transformed his wife. The only difference in the subsequent affairs was that they were even more experimental and took place at virtually all corners of the house. It is a practical miming of the series of porn she was watching. She would at most instance give Hawsawe 2000 riyal after a fulfilling sex debut and most were fulfilling. Condom was not considered anymore in their sex routine. Zahra had assumed that all immigrants in Saudi Arabia were healthier than the indigenes. For one she knew that immigrants were not allowed to renew their iqama (resident permit) without a compulsory medical test inclusive of screening for HIV and other sexually transmitted diseases. What she did not know was that some immigrants did not have iqama and Hawsawe was one of them. She found out only when Hawsawe demanded for her help to help him legalize his stay in Saudi Arabia. It was only after this that condom was introduced. Condoms were now routinely used in their sex. They were extremely cautious in neat picking every drop of the condom and its pack. Zahra never burdened herself with the neat picking it was for Hawsawe to do. One day while Hawsawe was busy cleaning the house after sex there was a knock on the door. With fear and not knowing who was knocking on the gate he ran out of the house. His duty did not include the interior of Khamdi mansion but the exterior only. In this process he forgot he had dropped the condom pack on the bedroom table with the intention of taking it out. His mind never went back to search through for he was in a hurry as he had an appointment with a travel agent to discuss his chances of immigrating to Canada. When Khamdi returned he found the condom pack. Khamdi continued to have ill feeling about Hawsawe and consulted his friend again. He was still assessing what he needed to do in the renovation. His friend advised him to add in his renovation a security camera, believing that if he could observe a little what went on in his absence he will become relaxed and quit his suspicion. Khamdi did not push the condom incident any further. He cared about his wife so much that in her pains from the burn wound he did not want her to worry about anything. He concluded on his own that Hawsawe and Aisha had stolen a moment in their room. He only blamed his wife for her closeness with Aisha for he believed it gave her the temerity to contemplate such act. Zahra felt guilty about the discovery of the condom but not the act. Her only planned defense, should Khamdi ask about the condom was to feign ignorance. Luckily for her he never asked.

She went for her daily wound debridement and was scheduled to see a plastic surgeon for her wound. Seeing the plastic surgeon he assessed the wound and told Khamdi that reconstructive surgery would not be possible for her because of her age and lax skin. She continued to dress her wound. With each session at the hospital came pains. Despite the analgesics she still felt a little pain. Each time she felt this pains she'd have to focus on her escapades but mostly the pain was a reminder that she shouldn't have done what she did. During those times, Hawsawe had taken an excuse to enable him meet up with the routines needed to get all his travel documents ready. He had lied to the Khamdis that he had lost a relative and would be involved in the running around for the burial and the subsequent ceremony that would be done in Nigeria. Aisha called him on phone to inform him about the condom incident and that made him to resolve to stay longer without coming to Khamdi mansion until he was sure the coast was clear. The renovation at Khamdi mansion lasted a few weeks. When it was completed the house wore a more modern look and its aesthetics was unrivaled. Besides the looks the house was now transparent for Khamdi could view its happenings from wherever he was. Once Zahra had fully recovered, she went to view her face in the mirror. She saw she had hyper-pigmented and hypo-pigmented patches scattered all over her face. It worried her that she had lived with a smooth pretty face but would have to die with a nightmare face. Looking at her face, made her angry so she resolved never to use the mirror and even avoided her usual video calls with her children. One day she broke her resolve and took a long look at the mirror, thinking of all that had transpired in her life she realized she had done something stupid like she had wanted. She resolved that she didn't need any more stupid deeds and decided she would quit her affairs and fantasy. Her plan was that the next time Hawsawe came to the compound after his long absence and senseless excuses that she would quit their contract. That time didn't take long to come. When the time came she wanted to have one last deed as her retirement. Hawsawe came in and since Khamdi was not around he went straight to meet Zahra in the bedroom. He informed her that he had made his papers to travel to Canada and decided to inform her before leaving. He had bought a bottle of whisky in the black market and he told Zahra that he would like it if they both could drink and merry since they would not see again. Zahra though she did not voice out her plans but had the same plans of never seeing Hawsawe again. Hawsawe went to the fridge and brought a bottle of coke and two glasses. He returned to the room, asked Zahra of her ordeal with the burns wound and they chatted like they were friends. He poured some spirits in each cup and added coke to fill up the cup. He passed one to Zahra and held his own. Hawsawe spoke to her of his joy that she had been instrumental to his recent upliftment. He thanked her for her generosity. They both toasted for his safe journey to Canada and drank the alcohol. Hawsawe reached for her where she was sitting on the bed, removed her clothes and they had sex. Eager to make their last sex memorable they had wild sex and the alcohol helped with all possible disinhibition.

# CHAPTER NINE

Khamdi was now tired of the routine checks of the house cameras. The first weeks he did this religiously and didn't find anything unusual. He felt the money he spent on security cameras where injudicious. He had forgotten to check the cameras for a while now. He was sitting in his office when it occurred to him to check what was happening at home. He saw that his wife was sleeping and Aisha was in her favorite place the aviary and tending the birds. He almost switched off the camera but just felt like seeing the history. He scanned back the previous days and there was nothing. Then he looked to see four days earlier. As he scanned through he could see Hawsawe entering the compound. He wondered why his wife never mentioned it. As he continued he saw he was entering the main building. Khamdi was becoming apprehensive but continued. Hawsawe was climbing the staircase. At this point his mouth was agape wondering what the black slave was going upstairs to do. He entered the bedroom and put hands in his pocket and brought out a bottle of alcohol. Khamdi screamed Kahul. He watched them seat and chat like lovebirds. He immediately switched off the camera and called his driver to get ready that he was coming out for them to leave. Then he switched the camera on again and by this time he was watching Hawsawe removing his wives cloth. He was screaming Hawsawe Hawsawe Hawsawe and as he continued to watch the sexually explicit video, his screams were getting louder. As he stood up to leave he screamed loudly and fell down on the floor. The driver could hear his scream and he came in and found his boss on the floor. He went out and called for help and he was taken to the hospital. By the time they reached the hospital he could not talk but only stare. He was diagnosed of having a stroke. News reached his wife and she came to the hospital. As Khamdi saw Zahra he struggled to talk but could not. Within this time he began to jerk and the hospital alarm was set off. After several minutes of code blue resuscitation Khamdi was declared dead. His burial was to take place immediately as required by Islamic laws and traditions. His daughters were informed of their fathers' deaths and all gathered and buried their father. The burial was over and Zahra was mourning her husband. Days later she was going through her husband's belongings sorting some out to be given away or destroyed. It was that day that she went through his phone and realized that the last activity in her husband's phone was her immoral affairs with Hawsawe. Aisha was still doing her usual chores when Zahra began to talk incoherently. As she came up she realized that her madam and friend had lost her mind. She was later taken to a mental home where she lived the rest of her life until her death.